FOUR VERY BIG BEANS

written by Lucy Floyd
illustrated by Lindy Burnett

HARCOURT BRACE & COMPANY

Orlando Atlanta Austin Boston San Francisco Chicago Dallas New York
Toronto London

I have four very big beans.
Mom gave all four to me.

But Grandma wanted one.
So now I just have three.

I have three very big beans.
But this one is for Sue.

Look! She wanted one!
So now I just have two.

I have two very big beans,
a **LOT** as you can see.

Did everybody get a bean?
This is so much for me!

Here, Mom! A bean for you!
And this one is for me!